For more than forty years,
Yearling has been the leading name
in classic and award-winning literature
for young readers.

Yearling books feature children's
favorite authors and characters,
providing dynamic stories of adventure,
humor, history, mystery, and fantasy.

Trust Yearling paperbacks to entertain,
inspire, and promote the love of reading
in all children.

OTHER YEARLING BOOKS YOU WILL ENJOY

JACKSON JONES AND THE PUDDLE OF THORNS
Mary Quattlebaum

GROVER G. GRAHAM AND ME, *Mary Quattlebaum*

MANIAC MONKEYS ON MAGNOLIA STREET/
WHEN MULES FLEW ON MAGNOLIA STREET
Angela Johnson

BUD, NOT BUDDY, *Christopher Paul Curtis*

THE WATSONS GO TO BIRMINGHAM—1963
Christopher Paul Curtis

THE DARK-THIRTY, *Patricia C. McKissack*

GLORIA RISING, *Ann Cameron*

JUNEBUG IN TROUBLE, *Alice Mead*

A PIECE OF HEAVEN, *Sharon Dennis Wyeth*

TROUBLE DON'T LAST, *Shelley Pearsall*

Jackson Jones
and
Mission Greentop

•••

MARY QUATTLEBAUM

A Yearling Book

Published by
Yearling
an imprint of
Random House Children's Books
a division of Random House, Inc.
New York

Yearling and the jumping horse design are registered trademarks of Random House, Inc.

Visit us on the Web! www.randomhouse.com/kids

Educators and librarians, for a variety of teaching tools, visit us at www.randomhouse.com/teachers

ISBN: 0-440-41957-3

Reprinted by arrangement with Delacorte Press

Printed in the United States of America

December 2005

10 9 8 7 6 5 4 3 2 1

OPM

To three inspiring teachers:
Sheila Cockey,
Deborah Green, and
Patricia Cheadle Patterson

CHAPTER ONE

• •

He's driving hard down the court. Ball under perfect control. Fake right, pivot. The way is clear. . . . YES! Ball headed for basket and . . . it's innnnn. Two points. Victory!

"You dreaming?" Reuben, my best friend, poked me.

I sighed. I could catch the far-off sounds of the game down the street. The mind picture of me quick-dribbling, shooting, scoring . . . disappeared.

No, I was rooted at Rooter's. Stuck in my plot at the community garden.

"Whatcha think of the name?"

I stubbed a weed. "Good for a monster."

"It'll be huge, green, and hated by all."

"Entire galaxies will tremble."

"The Unspeakable Z."

Reuben and I slapped skin. We had the perfect villain for our next comic strip.

Since third grade, Captain Nemo Comics has been our life's work. Reuben and I are an excellent team. I write; Reuben draws. I work fast; Reuben peers and puzzles, eyeballs and erases. Poke-turtle slow, that's Reuben. And finicky! But he does make Nemo look good.

Our favorite part is creating the villains. We make them mean, scary, and outer-space strange. Captain Nemo has tackled a six-headed Cerebral and a no-armed Flawt. Would the Unspeakable Z bring him down?

"Hey, you two," Mr. Kerring hollered from his fold-up chair. "You been on that weed for an hour. You think it's gonna pull itself up?"

Mr. K. is the oldest Rooter in the garden. And the best. His plot next to mine is laid out like a kingdom. Beet greens march in neat rows; leeks line up like soldiers. He can remember back to the garden's beginning—in 1944.

He can tell you how city folks grew food during World War II. "There was none of this running to 7-Eleven for chips," he humphs. Mr. K. calls Rooter's a victory garden.

Victory. I knew the word. It meant the drive to the basket. Slam dunk—and SCORE. The other team left in the dust.

Victory had nothing to do with a rosebush and squash.

The stuff surrounding me now.

People might have needed city gardens in the old days. But now? You can buy tomatoes and lettuce from Safeway. Gardens belong in the country. Deep in the country with cow muck and wasps.

Try telling that to my mama, though. She grew up in the country. And she *loved* every cow-flopping, bee-stinging minute. She worries that the city is no place for a boy.

So she made me a Rooter, last April. My tenth birthday, and I got . . . dirt. A patch of ground on Evert Street. Plot 5-1 rented in my name.

And there was no way I could give it back.

Mama's eyes had been so shiny-happy. "A little piece of country," she called my present. She had wanted to give me my own green spot.

So I dug and sowed, watered and waited. I dealt with puddles and thorns, a stingy bush with no roses. Now it was almost September, one week till school started. My crop had been mostly weeds—and trouble.

Here came some more.

Huge, green, and hated. The very thing Captain Nemo must conquer. The thing that made galaxies tremble.

The Unspeakable Z.

Zucchini.

Mailbags Mosely, who has the plot two over, laid it at our feet. He gave Reuben and me an easy smile. The man is as BIG as a buffalo— but that green vegetable, I swear, was as long as his shoes. Mailbags actually liked growing weird garden things. He passed them round like Hallmark cards.

Bang! went the garden gate. And more trouble blew through. Gaby and Ro Rivera, followed by their big sister, Juana. She was hollering at them in English and Spanish. Whatever the language, they paid no attention. They rushed through Rooter's like two wild winds.

We all live in the same apartment building. Juana, Reuben, and Mailbags are excellent neighbors. Gaby and Ro are not. Those two know only three volumes: loud, extra loud, ear-breaking. Their mission in life: to annoy.

The Riveras made straight for that zucchini. Gaby poked it with her toe.

Zucchini. It grows better than weeds at Rooter's. I have had it fried, stewed, sliced, and diced. I have had it baked, boiled, broiled, and breaded. I have had it up to here with zucchini.

"Jackson should get the zuke." Gaby grinned slyly. "His mama *loves* plants."

True. Our apartment is crammed with strange-sounding greens. Philodendrons, geraniums, begonias. But here's the embarrassing part: Mama chats with the things. Gives them pep talks. And they grow like the Amazon rain forest. Other kids have brothers, sisters, pets;

I live with a six-foot ficus. It towers by the phone, where, as Mama says, it has optimal light.

"But those plants are still growing." Juana spoke up fast. "Jackson's mama doesn't talk to *produce*."

Juana. She is one Super J. To the rescue, quick as Captain Nemo. Saving me from a meal of Unspeakable Z.

"Zucchini that size is too tough to fry," Mr. K. pronounced from his chair. "Make it into gazpacho."

"Mama doesn't know how to cook gaz— whatever," I said quickly.

"Neither does Miz Lady," Reuben said of his grandma. "Anyway, she's sick."

Mr. K. snorted. "Gazpacho's easy to make. Practically makes itself. In fact, young man"— he turned to Mailbags—"you hand that zuke to me."

Listen to the man bossing Mailbags! Huh, I know why Mr. K. has no weeds. He's commanded them to leave.

"Everyone's invited for dinner tomorrow

night." Mr. K. smiled upon us all. "Jackson, bring your mother."

I blinked and nodded.

As we hurried out the garden gate, I whispered to Juana, "What's gazpacho?"

"Soup," she whispered back.

Soup. That didn't sound so bad.

Right then, I should have sensed even more trouble. But I was too focused on Captain Nemo and the Unspeakable Z.

That's how trouble could creep up on me so easy. Creep up and whomp me on the head.

CHAPTER TWO

• •

Gazpacho.

Crammed with zucchini.

Cold.

Reuben and I stared into our bowls. Put down our spoons.

Mr. K. humphed while Mama and Mailbags spooned and sipped and paid compliments. Lucky Juana. She'd gone school-shoe shopping with Gaby and Ro. Lucky Miz Lady, at home with a cold.

"Now we have two Nemo villains," Reuben murmured. "Unspeakable Z and Gazpacho of Doom."

"They're closing in," I whispered. "Nemo's mission: *urgent*."

"Shhh," Mama said.

I slumped, glancing round the apartment. Brown couch, square TV, books stiff on a shelf. The one plant looked lonely without a green buddy.

Mr. K. lived in a building for old people. In this retirement home, Mama told me, the furniture came with the room. There were rules about what you could have.

Huh, no wonder the man dragged his lawn chair to Rooter's. In that mishmash of plots, no one cared what you grew.

"More soup?" Mr. K. peered from his kitchen.

No more, no way, I wanted to say.

Then I caught Mama's worry frown. It shows whenever she frets. Like when I talk back. Slip on my homework. Fill up on soda and chips.

So I decided to smooth on some strategy. My mission: to save myself from eating cold soup.

"Mr. K.," I said, "you ever hear how Mama rescued a ficus?"

Normally, I would never mention this tree.

Talk about embarrassing! Mama had hauled it out of the Dumpster in May. She had carted it home, cooed to it.

The thing had flourished. Like one of my weeds.

I plowed forward with my story. It was that or stare at cold soup. "Mama poked the soil and—"

"Overwatered," declared Mr. K.

"How did you know?"

Mr. K. shrugged. "Houseplant's number one problem."

"That's what Mama said," I told him. "That tree used to be so scrawny. Now it is looking *fine*."

Mama smiled; the worry frown disappeared.

I swelled, full of compliments. "You should be a doctor, Mama. A doctor for plants."

"You think so?" Mama asked.

I should have shut up then. I should have stopped trouble right there.

But I never realized trouble was coming— till it had bonked my head and kicked my behind.

So, like a fool, I said, "A doctor, yeah. For trees and flowers and stuff."

Reuben stared like I had lost my mind. Mr. K. shot me a sly look. Wise to my strategy, maybe.

But Mailbags chimed right in. "The boy could be right, Grace. There's no denying, things grow for you. A plant doctor—why not?"

Listen to Mailbags helping me out!

"Oh, I don't know." Mama shook her head. "I'm so busy with work."

"And with Jackson." Mr. K. hid a smile. Acting like I was a baby, with booties and drool.

"Huh," I said, stung. "If Mama wanted to study to be a plant doctor, well, I could take care of myself."

I would live to eat those words. Boiled, broiled, breaded, and baked.

• • •

Two days later, Mailbags knocked on our door and handed Mama a catalog. Handed? The man flourished that booklet like a gold candy box.

"A list of fall classes," he said. "The college offers a program in landscape design."

"What's landscape design?" I broke in. It sounded awful country.

"Oh, fixing up spaces with plants and trees. Making them look nice." Mama turned to Mailbags. "I don't think—"

"Listen to your mama, refusing my present." Mailbags winked at me. "Tell her it's not that hard, taking one class at a time."

Mailbags should know. He has been going to college for years. Toting mail during the day and listening to teachers at night. Why would a grown man *want* to go to school? It's a mystery to me.

"Wasn't that thoughtful?" Mama murmured when he had left.

I pointed out that Mailbags lived in our apartment building, on the first floor. "He didn't have to trudge through snow or sleet or ice," I said. "He brought that catalog in his little mail truck."

Mama smiled. "I mean, well, he thought those classes might be important—"

"But they're not," I interrupted. "You said you were busy."

"I am."

"You already know about flowers," I continued. "Plus, there's my garden. You can doctor that!"

Mama laughed.

But she didn't throw out the catalog. And later, after she had watered her green babies, patted the ficus, and wished me good night, I saw Mama pick up that catalog and start to read.

CHAPTER THREE

•••••••••••••••••••••••••

The idea must have taken root in Mama's mind then. And grown like the stubbornest weed.

But I was too busy to try pulling it out.

School had started, and I had a big problem.

Name of the problem: Blood Green.

Actually, his real name is Howard. But he changed it to Blood about a year ago—and punched any kid who called him anything different.

Blood, huh. I'd like to stick that boy in a Nemo strip. *Pow! Bam!* The captain would take care of him. Blood would be *yow*-ing all over the page.

But this was real life. And I was trapped.

Blood had been away for the summer. Camp, I heard. Torturing other kids while we kicked back for three Blood-less months.

Now he was back.

And, of course, he started his trash talk immediately.

Not in school, though. Blood is never mean where a teacher might hear. The boy has strategy. He waits till grown-ups are gone—and then he lets you have it.

"Hey, Bouquet Jones!"

I winced. Reuben, Juana, and I were taking in the b-ball game after school. Big guys playing on the Evert Street blacktop. Maybe they'd let us shoot a few hoops.

Gaby and Ro scratched in the dirt close by. Building an ant fort, they said.

"Barn Boy, you hear me?"

For Blood's information, I have never been within twenty miles of a barn. The only cow I've seen comes on a milk carton.

Listen to that hollering fool. Blood better watch out. I'm gonna hone my b-ball skills till I'm so fine I can dribble his bald head down any court and slam-dunk it through any hoop.

"Hey, Jones." Blood muscled up to me. "How's your little sweet pea?"

I stepped back, clenching my fists.

Ro wailed, "You *broke* our fort."

"You didn't answer my question, Jones." Blood rubbed his big shoe over Ro's little sticks.

"Stop it," Juana commanded.

"Sweet pea." Gaby snorted. "Jackson never grew one of *those.*"

"Yeah." Ro threw in his word.

Mama is always telling us big kids to watch out for the little ones.

But here was Miss Second Grade acting like she was watching out for me. And Mr. Kindergarten being all knight-in-shining-armor.

Pesky or protective. With Gaby and Ro, I don't know which is worse.

Blood kind of thickened and spread. Loomed over the little kids, crowded our space.

"Hey, Art Fart." He sneered at Reuben. "You got your pink crayon ready? Gonna draw a sweet pea for your spaceman?"

"You big stupid." Gaby rolled her eyes. "I *told* you—Jackson doesn't grow sweet peas."

She spoke very slowly. "He grows roses. Big. Red. All smelly good."

"Roses!" Blood threw back his head and laughed.

He laughed so hard, all over himself, that he opened a space.

Reuben and I squeezed by.

"Rose Jones!" Blood hee-hawed. "Big, red, smelly-good Jones."

Reuben and I picked up our pace. No sense sticking around. I could tell by his hunched shoulders that my man felt just like me.

Small. Silent. Filled up with shame.

Blood did that to a person.

The spring before, when I had gotten my plot, Blood had stepped up his usual mean-ness. On a mean scale of one to ten, he now measured thirteen. Smirking, name-calling, punching. Who knew why? Mailbags says Blood acts mean for a reason. He says that boy must be wanting—and wanting bad.

Well, whatever Blood was wanting, I wished he'd get it soon. And save my body some pain.

"Jackson!" Gaby hurried to catch up. She tugged on my sleeve. "I *rescued* you."

I tried to shake her off. "You didn't exactly rescue—"

"I did! I did!" exclaimed Gaby, skipping along.

"Me too!" shouted Ro, grabbing my other sleeve.

"Blood would have beat you up—*creamed* you!" hollered Gaby. "Did you hear me tell him off?" She sniffed. "That fool didn't know a rose from a sweet pea."

"Yeah." I was walking so fast I was puffing. I sure hoped the guys on the blacktop couldn't hear Gaby. Talk about embarrassing.

Juana poked me. "Jackson, you really should thank Gaby. She did help, after all."

Juana. Did I say she was a Super J? Know what the *J* stands for? *Justice*. Juana is *obsessed* with fairness.

But in what kind of just world does a fifth grader (me) have to thank a second grader (Gaby)? It would never happen to Captain Nemo.

Juana gave me her stubborn, you-know-I'm-right look.

"Thank you," I mumbled.

Reuben palmed Gaby's head, then Ro's. His way of saying thanks.

Gaby beamed. Now maybe she and Ro would forget the whole rescue.

Instead, Gaby continued to skip, happily singing all the way home: "Jackson grows roses. Jackson grows roses. Big, red, smelly-good ROSES."

The school year was not off to a good start.

CHAPTER FOUR

• •

But the year was bound to get better, right?

That evening Mama sat me down for what she called "a little talk."

Usually we only had these talks when I was in trouble. Or when my grades were bad.

I wracked my brain. Nope. I could safely say I hadn't bounced on, bounced off, or broken a thing in the past few weeks. As for grades, school had just started. We hadn't even had a pop quiz.

So I was cool going into our talk. "What's up?"

"Jackson," Mama said, "you've gotten so big. Ten years old."

Huh, I thought. Where was this headed?

"I looked into Mailbags's college."

College?

"And, well, I registered." Mama waved a piece of paper.

"You've already been to college," I pointed out. "Aren't you sick of school?"

"Not this school." Mama smiled, mentioning her classes. One on plants of North America, another on garden history.

Personally, I'd be snoring. But Mama was as happy as a well-tended ficus.

She told me she was in a special program since she already had a business degree. She wouldn't have to take as many classes.

Mama's worry frown appeared. "These classes aren't cheap, let me tell you. We'll have to watch our spending—" She hesitated. "And, Jackson, since I'll be working *and* going to school, I might need more help at home."

I looked round the apartment. How hard could that be? After all, I was double digits. The Big 1-0. Man of the House. We could do it, Mama and me.

21

"We can take turns fixing dinner," I said. "I can cook fish sticks. Soup from a can."

No more sliced, diced, baked, broiled zucchini. No more gazpacho.

Mama's eyes were so shiny-happy, I just had to tease. "Plant doctor." I rolled the words off my tongue. "You'll need a green ambulance."

• • •

Two weeks later I figured the first plants to need Mama's doctoring were mine. My garden sure looked sorry. In fact, the other twenty-eight plots looked bad, too. Even Mr. K.'s lettuce slumped.

Reuben and I watered the squash vines, lifted their leaves, let go.

Drooooooop.

Juana fingered a leaf. "What if you talked to 'em? Like your mama does."

"I'll *sing*," Gaby volunteered. She started in on that dumb Jackson-grows-red-roses song she'd made up two weeks before.

"That's okay," I said quickly. "I don't think singing will help."

"You're right." Mailbags moseyed over, carrying some tomatoes. "Those daisies are dying."

Dying? All that work and weeding that summer—and my plants were just giving up?

"Will you bury them?" Gaby asked.

Ro started to cry.

"Easy there, little man." Mailbags palmed Ro's head. "Fading's what happens this time of year. In a month or so, Jackson will have to cover his garden with straw, like a blanket. Bed it for winter."

I could tell Ro was listening hard, sucking his thumb.

"In winter the earth gets quiet," Mailbags continued. "It takes a rest."

I looked down. I felt sort of sad saying goodbye to these little green guys. We had been through a lot. Blisters, weeds, Blood. But we had pulled through. And it hadn't been all bad.

Mailbags smiled. "Come April, the whole thing will be back. You'll see. Squash, roses, weeds. Life moves in a circle. Things grow, die; others take their place."

I knew Mailbags was trying to toss out some wisdom. Talking that life-circle talk. But his words didn't make me feel better.

"It won't be the same," I said.

Mailbags stood quiet a moment. "You're right," he said. "Each year is different. You can plan and plant, but you can't know for sure. Gardens, well, they can surprise you."

"Like presents?" Gaby asked.

Mailbags smiled. "Sure. Have a tomato—gift from the garden. Probably the last of the season." He passed round the tomatoes, one for each kid. Tossed me another, for Mama.

As we stepped out the gate, Reuben nudged me. "Next year, if you wanted your garden . . . I could help."

"Me too." Juana nodded.

Did I want the garden again? Talk about work! Not to mention that plot's effect on my cool reputation. What b-ball ace grubs with worms? Messes with daisies?

I thought of Reuben's poke-poke-poke, careful, slow way of sticking seeds in the ground. Remembered Juana yanking weeds. I thought of Mama hurrying to the garden after work. We had chatted with Rooters. Watched green stems shoot through the dirt.

Yeah, mixed in with trouble had been some good garden stuff.

Besides, I'd invested a LOT of money and time in my rosebush. When the prickly thing FINALLY bloomed, I planned to be around.

"Listen to you." I grinned, spinning my tomato. "Two Farmers-in-the-Dell. Where's your pitchfork?"

Reuben fake-punched my arm.

"Next year, no zucchini," I promised as we moved down the sidewalk. "Not one single skinny green bit."

Reuben and I slapped skin.

"Hey, I almost forgot." Reuben dug into his backpack. "I finished the first Nemo panel. The one with Unspeakable Z."

"Boring!" Gaby sniffed. "Come on, Ro. Let's go look at *real* comic books."

The two shot down the street toward the drugstore.

"*Don't* squish tomato on anything," Juana yelled, picking up her pace. "And *don't* spin the racks."

I stopped to study Reuben's panel. Nemo was looking good. My man might take a loonng time to finish a strip. He might erase a million times. But his shading kept getting better. Look at the captain hacking that Unspeakable Z. The hairy vines choking the moon.

"Whatcha think?" Reuben asked.

"Weeelll." I drew out the word.

Reuben glanced down shyly.

"I think it's the best Nemo ever!"

"Yeah?"

"For sure."

Reuben took the paper from me, real careful. "I spent *hours* on those leaves. See the veins?"

"You know the plant drawings in Mama's books?" I tapped his panel. "This is just as good."

Then I heard a voice.

"Yo, Art Fart. And Rosy Red Jones."

Man, I hated that voice.

CHAPTER FIVE

• •

Blood Green materialized before us.

"You got something for me?" He eyeballed Reuben's panel.

My man hunched low over the paper. Like a daddy bird protecting his child.

"Leave him alone," I said.

Blood didn't even look at me. He reached out. Plucked the paper.

"Look at the wittle fwower." Blood's voice went all baby-squeaky. "And the wittle moon." He ran his thumb over Reuben's careful work. "But Rosy, where is the cow?"

"Cow?"

"The cow that jumps over the moon."

"Blood," said Reuben, "give it back."

"You want it?"

"Yeah."

Blood held the paper in both hands. Slowly, he started to tear.

Slowly, slowly, Blood tore down the middle. Doubled the paper, tore again.

Tossed the pieces into the air.

That's when—*whoosh!*—a tomato whizzed by his arm.

Whump! Another landed by his feet.

And a third smacked Blood in the chest.

What? Who? I glanced down the street.

Gaby, Ro, and Juana.

Gaby's aim had been off. Ro's, too.

Juana's had been perfect.

"You." Juana spat at Blood. "I wish I had more."

"Yeah!" yelled Gaby and Ro.

Juana grabbed the kids. Marched them into the drugstore. Her black hair waved, a Super J flag.

Blood just stood there, surprised. Seeds and juice dripped down his shirt.

That's when my survival instinct kicked in.

I ran.

Behind me, the pounding of feet. Reuben. His survival instinct was working, too.

I looked back once. Blood had disappeared.

Reuben and I didn't stop running till we reached our apartment building. His thoughts, I knew, were the same as mine.

Blood would pound us for sure.

Blood might poke Juana and the little kids. He might steal their lunches, call them names.

But he would come after Reuben and me. He couldn't look weak to other guys.

Reuben and I were dead meat.

We entered the elevator together; I pushed the button for the third floor.

"You okay?" I asked.

"Maybe." Reuben's voice trailed off.

We didn't say anything else, just nodded as we stepped off the elevator. Reuben headed to 316; me to 302.

I flung open my apartment door. Threw myself on the couch. Almost squished the tomatoes, still clutched in my hands.

I dropped them on the coffee table. Why

had Mailbags given us those things? He should have known they'd cause trouble.

And Juana? What was with her? Had Reuben and I asked for help? No! First Gaby and her Jackson-grows-red-roses comment to Blood. Then tomato-throwing Juana. Those Rivera girls—their rescues just made life dangerous.

I thought of Blood. His yellow shirt oozing red juice. Huh, he had asked for it. Tearing up Reuben's panel. That boy *lived* to be mean.

It was my turn to cook dinner that night. But I couldn't make myself move. My mind kept playing that picture of Blood being plastered. Fast-forwarding to him creaming me.

Should I tell Mama? She'd just worry and call Blood's mother. I shuddered. I'd seen what Blood did to kids who told.

Mama came out of her bedroom with her college stuff. These days she was always toting some book or tip-tapping on the computer. Before she started taking classes, I had cruised the Internet whenever I wanted. Checked out sports scores, got the scoop on players. Now I had to make an appointment for a three-minute search.

The computer might help me come up with a strategy, a way to keep Blood off my back.

"You're sweating." Mama gave me a kiss. "Play some basketball after school?"

I wished.

"And those tomatoes—big as beach balls!" Mama continued. "You slicing them for dinner?"

I shook my head.

"Putting them in a salad?"

"Right now," I said, "tomatoes are NOT my favorite vegetable. I'll scramble some eggs."

"Actually, the tomato is a fruit." Mama smiled. "It's even called the apple of love."

"Not by me," I grumbled.

Just then the phone rang. Blood had me so edgy, I jumped. The boy wouldn't call, I reasoned, reaching through the ficus for the phone. Huh, that tree was growing as big as a redwood. Why hadn't Mama rescued a teeny violet, say, or a stray basketball?

31

I pushed back a twig. "Hello."

Mr. Kerring answered.

Answered? The man *commanded* me to listen. He read aloud a letter from a company called Drane.

Even through the ficus rustling, I caught the news.

Seemed the tomatoes today were just the start of trouble.

And Mailbags's talk of garden surprises? Well, Rooter's was getting a surprise, according to the Drane and Company letter. And it wasn't good.

CHAPTER SIX

• •

I handed the phone to Mama. Tried to make sense of Mr. K.'s news.

No more garden.

Rooter's was going to be shut down. Plowed up. Developed.

An apartment building put there.

I thought of how my plot—number 5-1—had looked during the summer. Bees coming and going. Birds touching down. Flowers snug on their stems, beets fat in the ground. Okay, my rosebush had never bloomed. Maybe it was taking its time.

Now its time had run out.

Mama hung up, brushed past the ficus. Sat beside me on the couch.

"It's not right," I said.

"But it's legal." Mama leafed through the mail and opened our letter from Drane. "The company owns that land. We only rented it."

I leaned close, reading, too.

The letter was full of fancy words and polite "please's." I had to read it twice to figure its meaning. Drane and Company had bought Rooter's six years ago. They didn't want a garden, though. They wanted to build on that land. And now they wanted us out.

Six years. Huh. Mr. K. had been a Rooter since 1944. More than sixty years! I bet the company knew nothing about that land. To them, the garden was just a bunch of rental checks.

"Mr. Kerring will talk with a lawyer," Mama continued. "Maybe we can stop the development."

"Let's buy the garden!" I sat up straight. "Each Rooter can chip in."

But I knew that would never happen. It's hard enough to make your rent in the city. People didn't have money to rescue gardens.

"They plan to bulldoze in two weeks." I

scanned the letter again. "They want us to remove all our tools. I'll pick up the tomato stakes on Saturday."

"Bulldozing the garden." Mama shook her head sadly.

I glanced at the address at the top of the letter. Drane and Company was located downtown, on the same street as Mama's office.

Yeah, I remembered that street. Mama had hauled me to her office last year for Bring Your Daughter to Work Day. She said that sons, too, should see how the bills got paid. I had to wear my church shirt and drive in with her. I sat in her work cubicle. Spun in her chair. Checked out the people in suits.

But where were her plants?

"Not enough room," Mama had explained, perched on the edge of her desk. "And green leaves don't fit the color scheme." She waved. "Notice, please, the gray walls, gray ceiling, gray carpet."

"Tan computer," I said.

"My spot of color," Mama had joked.

Holding that letter, I guessed I could understand Mama better. Could see why she wanted to be a plant doctor so bad. I wondered if Drane and Company was as gray as Mama's cubicle.

I remembered the best part of visiting that downtown office. Mama had taken me to lunch. And she had let me order *two* chocolate puddings. "After all," she had said, laughing, "Bring Your Daughter to Work Day calls for celebration."

My mama, huh. She thinks she is one funny lady.

She wasn't joking now, though. The worry frown was deep between her eyes. She set down her college book. "You want me to make dinner tonight? So you can relax?"

"No way." I slid off the couch. "Didn't I promise scrambled eggs?"

Mama wanted to ease my sadness, I knew. But how could I relax with all this bad stuff? Blood tearing up Captain Nemo. Juana's tomato tearing into Blood. Mr. K.'s phone call. The Drane and Company letter. The garden soon to be bulldozed. Destroyed.

That was just today. What might happen tomorrow?

I sliced Mailbags's two tomatoes for Mama. Thick, the way she liked them. Served toast and scrambled eggs.

Mama ate fast, then headed to the computer. Her big paper was due soon, she said. She had to trace the history of a local garden.

Boring.

"Look at this Web site, Jackson." Mama clicked the computer mouse. "Tudor Place has a knot garden, one of the oldest in the country. Want to visit with me?"

And see a knot garden? Whatever that was. I *don't* think so.

"Got plans with Reuben that day," I answered quickly.

"Ah," said Mama. "I didn't mention a day."

Whoops.

"You do NOT want to visit the KNOT garden." Mama smiled. "So I will NOT expect you to come." She tugged my ear. "Like my plant humor?"

"Not," I said.

Mama laughed, then asked gently, "You okay? I can clean up."

No, Mama had to write about some boring

garden. I was the Man of the House. I'd do my part.

Besides, we had an agreement. Before Mama started classes, we used to clean up together. Now the cook also cleaned. This had been my idea, since I usually needed only one pan for canned soup, say, or fish sticks.

But tonight my strategy had backfired. That's what I got for cooking fancy. My scrambled eggs had stuck to the pan. Tomato bits were all over. Each pulpy seed reminded me of Blood.

I scraped and scrubbed, sponged and washed. Finally I turned out the kitchen light.

"Jackson," Mama called from the computer. "Could you give the ficus a drink?"

What was I, a guy Cinderella? But I didn't say a word. Mr. Helpful Man of the House filled a jug and lugged it over.

By the phone, the tree kind of drooped. Maybe feeling a little lonely. Mama was spending so much time with her book plants that she was forgetting her real ones. No more pep talks or songs. Just a quick "hi" when she watered.

"You think you've got it bad," I murmured, patting the ficus. "I know a whole garden that's gonna be bulldozed. And a person that's gonna get creamed."

I meant to cheer up the tree. But it only drooped worse.

CHAPTER SEVEN

• •

Over the next few days, the ficus and I spent a lot of time together. I was always dodging its leaves to answer the phone.

Most of the calls came from Mr. Kerring. I could hear the worry each time he barked a command.

He told Mama and me about his talk with a lawyer, who said there was nothing we could do. He had talked to another lawyer, who gave the same answer. The garden could be sold, bulldozed, developed. Drane and Company's action was legal.

That still didn't make it right.

What might save the garden? I thought and

thought. Tried to come up with a strategy. We needed one soon.

Another strategy I needed soon: a way to save myself. And Reuben.

Word of the tomato incident had spread through school faster, well, than Juana's throw. These days kids snickered whenever Blood swaggered by. They whispered, "Tomato Head." Blood's bullying had caught up with him.

And he was waiting to catch up with me.

Blood had strategy, though. He started spreading on niceness, thick as jam. "Hello, Jackson" in the halls. "How's it going?"

The boy was as friendly as a welcome wagon.

He wouldn't strike at school, I knew. Too many teachers. Too easy to get caught.

No, Blood had gone underground. Like a mean snake in a burrow.

But Reuben and I refused to be gophers. Two gophers waiting for that snake to strike. We had our own strategy: going to and from school a different way each day. If he couldn't predict our movements, Blood couldn't jump us.

Captain Nemo might fight his villains. He'd punch the Flawt, whomp the Cerebral, tackle the Unspeakable Z. But this was real life. Reuben and I tried to avoid the enemy.

On Saturday, I was still in avoidance mode. Reuben and I had worked out a plan. I'd go to the garden early to clear out my stuff, before the bulldozers came. Blood would still be asleep. Then I'd meet Reuben back at our apartment building. I'd pick up my b-ball, and we'd head for the blacktop. Shoot hoops for the rest of the morning. If Blood found us, he might launch some mean names, but he wouldn't touch us. Too many people around.

At seven o'clock, I was moseying down the street. Turning the corner onto Evert.

Morning mist silvered the garden. A breeze rustled through. Two birds started a chirp conversation.

That's when I saw them.

Big. Red.

My rosebush had finally bloomed.

I opened the gate, hurried over.

Four roses! From a thorny stick to a blooming beauty—that bush had come a long way. Wait till Mama saw it.

"You stubborn thing." I tapped a flower. "Deciding to look nice—right before being bulldozed."

"Got yourself some roses," came a voice.

Talk about embarrassing. Had the person heard me? I was as bad as Mama, talking to plants!

Hunkered in his neat plot was Mr. Kerring. Surrounded by two buckets, three plastic bowls, about twenty paper cups.

His garden was full of holes.

Mr. K. shifted stiffly, peering at me. He looked like an elderly groundhog.

"June roses are a dime a dozen," Mr. K. humphed. "Everything blooms in summer." His spade scratched into the earth. Dig. Dig. Dig. He slowly filled one of the bowls.

"But a fall rose is special," he continued. "Coming right before winter. Promising spring."

I didn't want to remind Mr. K. about the next spring. When it came, Rooter's would lie under some building.

Mr. K. stopped, resting a moment. Smoothed back his wispy hair.

Quickly I reached for the spade.

Mr. K. held tight. "I can do it," he barked.

I held on.

"Okay, but just for a minute," he grumbled. "Treating me like an old man."

Dig, dig, dig. I filled one of the buckets.

Dig, dig. I started on a bowl.

The sun was warm on my back, the dirt rich and black. An earthworm slithered away.

"I've worked this plot since I was ten," Mr. K. said suddenly. "My grandma taught me how to build up the soil, how to stake a tomato. No, Jackson." He shook a finger. "You'll get a blister holding the spade that way."

"Uh-huh," I said, continuing to dig. I tried to picture Mr. K. as a boy. No wrinkles, no gray hair. Bossy as ever. Somehow, though, his commands didn't crab me as much. His words slid off me like rain off a leaf.

"Things were different back then," Mr. K. went on. "Victory gardens all over the city. On balconies, in windows. Every patch of dirt held some green. Americans had to grow their own food during the war. We had to free up factory food for the troops."

He cut me a sly look. "I remember a LOT of zucchini."

"Some things don't change," I replied.

Mr. K. chuckled. "Turnips. Parsnips. Rhubarb. You ever eat rhubarb without sugar?"

Rhubarb? Sounded like a villain for Captain Nemo.

"Sour." Mr. K. stuck out his tongue. "And sugar was rationed. My grandma used to stick that nasty stuff in a pie. Call it dessert."

I glanced round the garden as I dug. Brown and dry, most of it. Some pansy faces still shone, though. Marigolds still hung out their colors. My roses were full and red. Strange to think of plants and people coming and going for years on this one patch of ground.

Suddenly I stopped. Mr. K.'s garden had gone from the prettiest in Rooter's to the ugliest. Even my weed jungle looked better. The man now had a gopher city.

"Mr. K.," I said slowly, "what are we doing?"

His eyes turned stubborn. Like Juana's when she feels she's right. "It's my dirt," he said. "I prepared it, fertilized it. I set out earthworms I bought myself."

I could see it now: me and Mr. K. arrested for vandalizing. For stealing Drane and Company soil.

"The whole thing will be plowed up." His old voice cracked. "In a few weeks, this will be gone. You think I'm gonna waste this rich dirt?"

Mr. K. protectively gathered his bowls. "I'm gonna start an indoor garden."

I thought of Mailbags's talk about seasons. How earth rested in winter, grew more plants in spring. Mr. K.'s dirt would keep creating—even when Rooter's disappeared.

"Mr. K.," I said, "can I use a cup?"

He smiled. "Gonna grow your own zucchini?"

"Only if you eat it." I smiled back. Knelt in my plot. Dig, dig, dig.

I filled one cup for me.

Dig, dig. I filled four extra. For Reuben,

Juana, Mama, Mailbags. Dirt from Plot 5-1. Guaranteed to grow the city's best weeds.

I ran my sleeve over my face. Talk about hard work.

But the hardest part was still to come.

Mr. K. planned to trundle his dug-up plot home in a teeny wire cart. In this rickety basket with two skinny wheels.

But two buckets, three bowls, and twenty dirt-filled cups didn't fit.

I sighed and hoisted the buckets. Mr. K. tugged his cart.

We struggled down the street. Slow as two ancient turtles.

Of course, when we passed the b-ball blacktop, the big guys had to comment.

"Jackson! Look at you."

"All that dirt—you making a cornfield?"

I gave them a nod. Trudged on.

The sun was getting higher in the sky. And I was getting nervous. I was late to meet Reuben.

Blood would already be on the move.

I sure didn't want to see Blood. Not hauling

two buckets, like some baby Jack-and-Jill rhyme. Not with Mr. K.'s squeaky cart.

I picked up the pace.

If I had known what was waiting, I would have slowed down. Way down.

Huh, if I had known what was waiting with Reuben, I would have stopped. Turned around. Gone back. Buckets, squeaky cart, and all.

Chapter Eight

• •

Waiting for me were noise and confusion.

I had just dropped Mr. K. off at his place. Mr. K. and his gallons of dirt. In a few weeks, when the first seeds sprouted, his one plant would have company. LOTS of company.

Mr. K. turned stubborn when I asked about his building's rules. "They got rules on wall color, carpet, the number of pictures," he grumbled. "But I never read one word about dirt."

Climbing the steps to my apartment building, I flexed my fingers. Those five paper cups were hard to hold. And a blister was starting to form. It better not mess with my blacktop action. After being Farmer-in-the-Dell all morning, I needed a b-ball game.

But when I pushed open the door of our building . . . noise pushed back at me.

Gaby and Ro were stomping round the lobby.

Reuben screeched his marker on a big square of paper.

Juana directed his writing.

Uh-oh. Juana had that J-for-justice look in her eyes. And there was no basketball in sight.

When they saw me, Gaby and Ro rushed over. "We're practicing!" they yelled.

I glanced at the finished signs. Reuben's letters were large, black, and clear.

Save the Garden

Root for Rooter's

Mother Nature Now

"Jackson," Juana greeted me. "Listen, I've got a plan."

● ● ●

That's how I found myself back on the sidewalk, headed to Rooter's.

This time toting a sign.

Before setting out, I'd had a chance to stash my dirt-filled cups in my apartment, under the ficus. "Wish me luck," I whispered to the tree.

Yeah, I was going to need LOTS of luck. Juana's plan called for a protest march.

And that girl wanted to put her plan into action *immediately*. No waiting for Mama, who'd gone to the library. No waiting for Mailbags, who was delivering Saturday mail. No calling any of the other Rooters.

"But they're part of the garden, too," I pointed out.

Besides, I thought, a few grown-ups might give our protest some dignity. I'd seen marches on the TV news. Grown-ups shouting, waving signs. Would people pay attention to kids?

"We need to march *now*." Juana tossed her black hair. "The bulldozers come next week."

Seemed to me Juana was rushing things.

Super J bent on righting a wrong. I wished some of Reuben's slow, careful style would rub off on her.

"What do you think?" I whispered to Reuben.

"Juana thinks people will join us," he whispered back. "She thinks they'll want to help the garden."

"But what do *you* think?"

Reuben shrugged. "I think it's impossible to stop Juana."

Juana lined us up, passed out signs. "Too bad we don't have matching T-shirts, with fists."

"Pink ones," shouted Gaby.

"Blue," yelled Ro.

I rolled my eyes. Who would notice five kids? No matter what we wore.

You'd be surprised.

One part of Juana's strategy worked fine. People did notice.

"Look at those kids!"

"So cute."

"What garden you trying to save?"

"Rooter's on Evert Street." Juana proudly hoisted her sign.

Yeah, we hadn't even reached the garden and we were being noticed.

One person who noticed: Blood Green.

He fell into step beside me. The only one to join our march.

I hadn't seen Blood this close since the tomato incident. Man, the *size* of his chest. No wonder Juana hadn't missed. The boy was as big as a battleship.

Blood glanced at my sign, reading slowly: "Mother . . . Nature . . . Now."

That stupid slogan. Juana's idea.

"Mother . . . Nature . . . Now." Blood drew out each word.

I knew how Blood's brain worked. He'd add Mother Nature to his list of mean names. He'd holler it at the blacktop, at school. Rose Jones. Barn Boy. Mother Nature.

Reuben and Juana moved closer in case I needed help.

"You're crowding me." Blood's eyes narrowed. "Don't want me in your parade?"

"This is not a parade," Gaby corrected. "It's a *protest*."

"A big one," said Ro. "To save the garden."

"Five kids?" Blood sneered. "You look like fools." He snapped his fingers under Juana's nose. "But I can help."

"We don't want your help." Juana's jaw was set.

"But I wuv wittle fwowers." Blood pouted. "And I know just what to do."

With a flip of his big hand, he was gone.

That syrup-sweet meanness was worse than his usual style.

Reuben cocked his head. "Blood's messing with us."

"Come on," Juana said. "He can't jump us all."

No, Blood wasn't planning on jumping us. He wanted something worse. Something, I bet, that would last a loonng time.

"Garden! Garden!" Gaby and Ro chanted as we meandered down Evert Street.

Rooter's stretched out. Dots of color mixed with brown stems. Purple pansies, yellow marigolds, my four red roses.

Toting our signs, we circled the entire garden.

Circled again.

"Garden! Garden!" hollered Gaby and Ro.

Neighbors waved. A dog barked. Birds chirped, fell silent.

No one joined us.

"My feet hurt," whined Ro.

"Then sit and shout," said Juana.

"I'm *thirsty*."

"So, get a drink." Juana continued to march.

Gaby and Ro scampered to the faucet. They turned it on, grabbed for the hose. The long thing whipped like a snake.

Whooooosh.

Water hit my face, shirt, jeans.

"Whoops," said Ro.

"Sorry," Gaby said, then giggled. "Jackson peed his pants."

"You okay?" Reuben asked.

I nodded, wiping my eyes.

"Oh, Jackson." Juana frowned at my dripping clothes. "Now we'll have to stop or you'll catch a cold."

"Hey, it wasn't my fault."

Juana swept us with her Super J look. "We return tomorrow."

Gaby and Ro groaned.

Thunk. Thunk. The quick-dribble sounds of a b-ball game reached me. I sighed. Reuben and I never had made it to the blacktop.

"What are you sighing about?" Juana asked.

I shrugged, trying to wring out my shirt.

"There," Juana said. "You sighed again."

"Did not."

"Did too."

"Juana," I said, "it's like you're ob*sessed.* On a twenty-four-hour rescue or something." I put on a deep Captain Nemo voice. "We return tomorrow. Prepare for action. All ready for mission . . . Mission Greentop."

"More like Browntop." Reuben glanced at the garden.

Juana crossed her arms. "Well, if *you* want to quit . . ."

I crossed *my* arms. Couldn't Juana tell that her plan wasn't working?

"What happens tomorrow?" I asked.

"In your spaceman comic"—Juana sniffed—"things change all at once. This is real life. A protest can take a long time."

But it turned out Juana was wrong.

Things can change in a day, an hour, a minute.

Rattle. Splutter. Coming down Evert.

Things were about to change.

CHAPTER NINE

• •

A black car pulled to the side of the street. Coughed to a stop.

A guy jumped out. "Nathan Aramack. Local news," he announced, striding through the gate.

Someone had called the media.

Reuben eyed Juana nervously.

"Not me," she said.

Nathan Aramack dropped his pen. Scrambled for it in the squash vines.

We stared curiously. This was a news guy? He seemed awful young and gawky, with his camera string twisted round his neck. Where was that silver-haired man from the evening news? Where were the big TV cameras?

Finally Nathan recovered his pen. "Jackson Jones?"

"That's me," I answered, surprised.

"You called about a protest march." Nathan dug out a notepad. "Something endangered."

"I didn't."

"Your name Jackson?"

"No," I said. "Yes. What I mean is"—I shifted uneasily—"I'm Jackson, but I didn't call."

"You're all wet."

I sighed, not wanting to explain.

Nathan craned his neck. Maybe searching for hidden protestors. Or for something endangered. A panda or bald eagle.

"This is the march? Five kids?" He capped his pen in disappointment. Turned to leave.

Stepped right into one of Mr. K.'s holes.

After we helped him up, Nathan told us why he had come. He was a college student working at the news station once a week. The call about the protest had come in, and the big news guys had sent him to investigate. Thus far, our protest was his only story.

It hit me then.

This was the work of Blood Green.

He had called the news station, pretending to be me. He wanted the media to see us— and decide our march was worthless.

He wanted to prove that saving the garden was stupid.

Blood was making us into fools.

"Excuse me." I stepped my wet-shoe self closer to Nathan. "There are five of us, yeah. But the number's not important. What's important—" I waved my arm, flinging drops. "Whoops. Sorry." I waited while Nathan wiped his face. "What's important is this garden. Sixty years old."

"Next week," Juana added, "it will be gone."

Nathan started asking questions then.

Questions about the garden's history. The other Rooters. Drane and Company's actions.

We led Nathan round the garden as he wrote and snapped photos. I talked about victory gardens, rhubarb, leeks. Explained how good soil creates, year after year.

Luckily Nathan didn't ask any questions about Mr. K.'s holes. I didn't want the old man to get into trouble for taking soil—even though he claimed it was his.

I pointed to my four fall roses.

They appeared on TV that night.

Huh, my thorn tree sure looked important, there on the evening news.

The TV picture also held Gaby and Ro, grinning. Reuben clutched a sign. Juana fixed the viewer with her Super J gaze. I was as wet as a fish, with two fingers raised. Two fingers forked into a *V*.

V for *victory*. Victory garden, that is.

The silver-haired newsman mentioned our protest. Described our mission. The garden got two minutes, tops.

It was over so fast, I thought probably no one saw.

Then the phone started ringing.

It rang.

And rang.

And rang.

I got a workout that evening, ducking under the ficus to answer the phone.

At the computer, Mama smiled. "Who knows what might happen now?"

The phone kept ringing.

Mailbags congratulated us on our strategy.

Mr. K. asked about Drane and Company.

"Prepare yourself, Jackson," he barked. "This is bad publicity for a hotshot company. They're going to be tough on you."

When I hung up, I sat under the ficus awhile. Mission Greentop had gotten complicated.

What would Drane and Company say when they called?

And what would I say to them?

CHAPTER TEN

• •

By the next morning, Mama and I were sick of the phone.

Ring. Ring. Ring. Mama couldn't study. I needed a break from answering questions.

Juana had been one of our earliest callers. She told me she was busy with church stuff all day.

"But we'll march in the evening," she promised. "Bring a flashlight."

Mission Greentop would continue.

I sighed, spooning my cereal. Juana was zooming ahead, as usual. How would a night march help the garden? Who could see us in the dark?

"You feeling stressed, Mr. Celebrity?" Mama

asked. "Want to visit Tudor Place with me? A little piece of country in the city."

Mama made her research trip sound fun—but I knew better. When I was little, Mama was always dragging me to green spaces. Big, little, indoors, outdoors. We wandered through teeny city squares and walked down too-long forest trails.

Mostly the trips had been okay. I learned more about poison ivy than I'd ever wanted to know. But when I turned eight, I needed weekends for guy stuff: planning Captain Nemo with Reuben, shooting hoops, reading the Sunday comics. Mama had a whole jungle at home. That was enough green for me.

But at least going with Mama today would save me from the phone. A knot garden. Why not?

On the drive through the city, Mama talked about Tudor Place. The land was purchased in 1805, she told me, and the mansion completed in 1816. The first owner had been the stepgranddaughter of George Washington. The same family had owned Tudor Place for six generations.

"Mama," I teased, "you sound like their Web site."

She laughed as she parked the car. "I printed it out." She patted her folder. "I knew you'd have LOTS of questions."

We passed through the gate and—just like that—the city disappeared. No traffic, no sirens, no honking horns.

My first thought: Reuben had to see this.

A garden laid out so perfect. Careful as a Nemo drawing by Reuben.

The teeny hedges were clipped like poodles and lined up just so, making fancy designs. The hedges seemed to cross over each other, like the neat way Reuben looped his shoe-laces. I could picture old-time rich people strolling around. Checking out the time by the sundial.

This was the famous knot garden.

Mama and I moseyed down white gravel paths. We sniffed the boxwood, fingered the holly, and caught the *trickle-trickle* of the lion fountain. We sat in the teahouse for a while, like old-time rich people, and took in the huge, plush lawn.

"When you finish your classes, you gonna doctor big gardens like this?" I asked.

Mama shook her head. "I want to work with small spaces, outdoors and indoors," she replied. "Places where people live and work. Nursing homes, schools, offices. People need green, peaceful spots."

Huh, Mama's gray office better watch out. It was due for some color.

"And I want to start my own business," Mama added.

"With a plant stethoscope?" I teased. "And a green ambulance?"

Mama smiled. "Exactly."

We found a tulip poplar tree, one hundred feet tall. And rosebushes tucked close to the mansion. All planted by the first owners, Mama told me.

They were two hundred years old.

It gave me a weird feeling to think of my thorn tree living that long.

Then I remembered: It couldn't. The bulldozers were coming next week.

• • •

We drove home in silence. Dark clouds gathered over the tight-packed buildings, the few city trees. "We're in for a storm," Mama said.

I barely noticed. I was thinking of Rooter's. That funny mishmash of twenty-nine plots.

It might not be finicky like a knot garden.

But, in its way, it was just as fine.

Mama had fed me so many facts about Tudor Place that I felt like their Web site. The house and gardens were a historic museum, she had told me. The knot garden was protected. No one could ever bulldoze or build on it.

I knew about other safe land, too. The government protected those forests Mama and I had visited. Those forests with that nasty poison ivy. Called them national parks. Those parks had LOTS of land and trees, even whole mountains.

I just wanted to save a small patch.

CHAPTER ELEVEN

• •

By the time Mama and I got home, my brain felt like a knot garden. My thoughts were jumbled into a maze. And I still hadn't come up with a good rescue strategy.

But Juana had.

That girl must have been training her Super J eyes on our door. She materialized as soon as Mama unlocked it.

"Ready?" She hitched her backpack.

"Juana," I said, "I don't think a night march—"

"You're absolutely right," she replied seriously. "I have a better idea."

What now? I wanted to discover the details

before I dove into the plan. "Tonight's not good." I tried to stall. "It's my turn to cook—"

"Oh." Mama broke in as Juana's face fell. "You two go ahead. I'll make dinner. Jackson, can you be back in an hour?"

"Sure," Juana agreed for me.

"Sooner if it rains?"

"Sure." Juana grabbed my sleeve and trotted me down the hall. Her backpack clinked and clanked.

"Easy, easy." I smoothed my jacket. "What's that noise?"

The backpack clanked even louder as Juana handed it to me. "Listen, Jackson." She punched the elevator button. "This is the plan."

• • •

For the second day in a row, I headed to Rooter's. This time I wasn't toting a sign. I was carting a backpack.

Full of candles in teeny glass cups.

Juana had bought twenty-four candles from her church. Her plan: to hold a vigil.

"What's that?" I asked, clanking down Evert.

Juana explained that a vigil was like a wish or a prayer. People stood together and thought the same thing. Maybe they wanted world peace or they mourned someone dead.

"In our case," Juana said, "people hope to save the garden."

"*What* people?" I said. "Where's Reuben? Where's Gaby and Ro?"

"You know Mr. Careful." Juana unlatched Rooter's gate. "Reuben won't go anywhere with the kids and a box of matches. He said Rooter's would burn for sure."

She unzipped the backpack. "And Gaby and Ro refused to come. They figured I was going to church with these candles."

"So we have a two-person vigil?"

"It's a start." Juana handed me the first candle. "People will join us, you'll see. Tomorrow we'll call all the Rooters."

I didn't see how candles and wishes could help the garden. But I kept my mouth shut. Juana had paid for those lights with her own money. I figured I could stand and hope for a while.

Juana and I set out the twenty-four candles. Funny how they could hang so heavy in the backpack—but form only one little row.

"Never mind," Juana said. "The flames will glow like a . . . a sign of hope."

The hard part, though, was making them glow. A breeze blew out each flame. We tried three times before we succeeded in lighting one candle.

Great. Twenty-three to go.

Finally the last candle flamed. Juana and I stepped back, surveying our work. The row of soft lights shone.

I had to admit: The teeny candles did look hopeful, flickering there.

That's when I realized our mistake. Juana and I had focused on the ground—and forgotten to check out the clouds.

"Uh-oh," I said, "I felt a raindrop."

Boom. Thunder.

The skies suddenly opened.

• • •

For the second day in a row, I trudged home in wet clothes. Only this time I clanked.

Juana and I had thrown the drenched candles into the backpack.

"At least we tried," I said when we reached our building.

Juana shouldered the backpack. "We return tomorrow," she said.

I sighed. Juana sure was determined. That's great in a superhero, like Captain Nemo. But in a real person . . . I mean, I appreciated Juana's help and all. I just wished she'd mix some careful with her take-charge style.

When I opened my apartment door, though, I forgot about vigils and rain. A spicy smell tugged me into the kitchen. Pizza! Mama was always talking about the expense of delivery pizza. "We can pick it up ourselves," she would say. "We can make our own."

And now she had surprised me.

Her way of saying thanks, I bet. She was grateful that I cooked and cleaned and watered the ficus so that she could tip-tap on the computer.

I swelled, full of good feeling. Yeah, Mr. Man of the House.

I prepared myself for a flat, steaming box.

Instead Mama trotted out . . . four English muffins. They were dabbed with red sauce and cheese strips.

Fake pizza.

My hungry stomach growled like a Saint Bernard.

"What's wrong, Jackson?" Mama set down the pan. "I thought you liked pizza."

"That's *not* pizza," I said.

"Well, it's dinner," Mama replied. "I've got too much work to cook anything else."

"You always have too much work," I muttered.

"That's not true," Mama said. "What about today?"

I pointed out that a knot garden wasn't exactly Disney World. We had visited because Mama was researching a paper. It wasn't like she had planned a fun day for me. I reminded her of all my cooking and cleaning.

"And you're neglecting your plants," I finished. "Look at the poor ficus. I'm the one talking to it."

Mama led me, sopping wet, to the couch. "You've been very helpful, Jackson," she said.

My stomach rumbled.

"I never meant for you to become a . . . a guy Cinderella."

I squirmed. "It's not that bad."

At least I didn't have to mop floors or wrestle an old-time stove. We had a car, not a pooping horse. With her luck, Cinderella was probably stuck pruning the family knot garden. I'm glad I didn't live in the past.

The idea hit then. A way to save Rooter's.

My strategy wasn't brilliant.

But maybe it would work.

I jumped off the couch. "Can I use the computer?"

"I thought—" Mama paused, puzzled. "I thought you wanted to talk about your chores."

"Oh, yeah," I said. "Can we do that later?"

Right now I was on a mission.

CHAPTER TWELVE

• •

Three days later, I was staring at gold words on a door.

Drane and Company.

I tugged at my church shirt. Set down my briefcase, an old one of Mama's. Shook the wet off my jacket hood.

For the past three days, it had rained. Gray, steady. Rain, rain, rain. Juana had to call off all marches and vigils. And the bus ride downtown this morning—downright dangerous. All those poking umbrellas.

On the sidewalk, I had splish-splashed through puddles. Passed the building where Mama worked. Good thing her cubicle didn't have windows. If she caught me skipping school . . .

I had memorized the address I was searching for—the address on the letter about bulldozing Rooter's.

I read the door's gold words again.

Drane and Company.

I swallowed. Tried to think what Nemo would do. The captain would zoom in, laser blazing.

The captain never felt fear.

Maybe I should have brought Reuben, my slow, careful bud. Or Juana, with her take-charge style. But, for sure, I'd get in trouble for skipping school. I couldn't bring them down, too.

And my new strategy . . . I wasn't sure it would work.

That's why I hadn't told a grown-up. Mama, Mailbags, Mr. K.—they would say we needed lawyers and more time to plan.

And there wasn't time. The rain might postpone the bulldozing. But not for long. I bet Drane and Company would act quickly.

I hoisted my briefcase.

Stepped into an office that was nothing like Mama's.

The carpet was thick and blue, the walls a soft white. I felt upside down. Standing on sky, surrounded by clouds.

Suddenly a voice spoke from a desk. "You selling something?"

I jumped. "Me? I'm here to see Mr. Drane."

"Mr. Drane?" The receptionist cocked her head. "This should be . . . interesting. What's your name? Company?"

"Er, Mr. Jones," I said, trying to sound grown-up. "My company—I guess it's Rooter's."

"You have an appointment, Mr. Jones?"

I shook my head. "But my, um, business is urgent."

The receptionist spoke into her phone.

"Go right in," she finally said. "Second door to the left."

This was it. My heart dropped. Landed somewhere near my stomach. What if Mr. Drane had seen me and Rooter's on the news?

Bad publicity for the company, Mr. K. had warned me. They'll be hard on you.

"Mr. Jones," said a voice as I opened the door.

"Why"—the voice rose—"you're a child!"

And Mr. Drane was a woman.

Okay, we were both surprised.

With her poofy hair, Amelia Drane didn't look like the usual bad guy. She wasn't a scary Flawt or an Unspeakable Z. When she asked me to sit, a smile slid briefly across her face. Her perfume hung in the air like a net.

Turned out Amelia Drane had seen Rooter's on TV—but didn't think our march was important. She hadn't even remembered my name.

"A protest that lasted one day?" she asked briskly.

"There was a vigil, too," I tried to explain, "but the rain—"

"And *you* are the Rooter's representative?" she interrupted.

I could tell she didn't think much of a kid representative.

"Mr. Jones." Amelia Drane spoke from behind her desk. "I run a business. That little

78

piece of land has been losing money for years. The taxes are enormous."

She spoke slowly, as if I wasn't very smart.

I started feeling mad. But I held back. Amelia Drane didn't know what I knew.

Besides, Mr. K. had given me LOTS of practice in handling bossy people. I let her words slide off me. Drip, drip, drip. Like water off a leaf.

"Finally there's a chance to build," continued Amelia Drane. "Tell me why I shouldn't."

Her desk hulked before me like a fort.

That's when I opened my briefcase.

CHAPTER THIRTEEN

· ·

I guess I should say that's when I *tried* to open my briefcase.

One of the latches was stuck. I fiddled and poked and pried.

Amelia Drane clicked her nails on the desk. I could tell she didn't think much of Rooter's, my briefcase, me.

"There!" I shouted as the latch popped free.

"Mr. Jones"—she made a big show of checking her watch—"I have an appointment at eleven."

"Wait, wait." I frantically pulled out papers. Handed her a huge stack.

Amelia Drane glanced at a few pages. "This

is information on historic places," she said, "with the National Park Service."

"Rooter's has *historical significance*." I had memorized the key words. "It's a victory garden, more than sixty years old. It should be preserved."

Rooter's was like that famous knot garden. It was the past, still alive.

Amelia Drane raised her brows.

"You should give Rooter's to the government," I continued. "You just have to fill out some forms."

Amelia Drane sucked in her breath. Then she spoke *very* slowly. She must have thought I was an idiot.

"I won't fill out any forms."

"Then I will," I said.

Amelia Drane opened her mouth. Struggled.

"You?" she finally got out.

I smiled.

Over the past three days, when Mama wasn't on the computer, I had searched, scanned, downloaded. I had read LOTS of teeny print.

Most of it was confusing. But I could understand some.

A place with historical significance can be reviewed by the National Park Service. Maybe protected forever. And if the owner does not ask for a review, someone else can.

"Maybe not me exactly," I explained to Amelia Drane. "But my mama. Or a lawyer. Anyway, there's no bulldozing till after a review."

"It could be months till we start!"

"Or maybe never," I said.

Amelia Drane eyeballed me. She was flipping through strategy fast.

Her smile slipped back into place. "A new apartment building means homes for more people."

"You can build on other land."

"I've seen that garden. It's full of weeds."

I winced. Probably my weeds. I quickly tossed out some of Mailbags's life-circle talk. "The garden's fading now," I explained. "Soon we'll bed it for winter. Just watch, the flowers will return in the spring."

I crossed my arms. Maybe Juana's Super J had rubbed off on me. "The garden could be good publicity for you—or bad," I said. "There's a TV guy interested in what happens." I thought of Nathan Aramack, with his twisted-string camera.

Amelia Drane paused.

I waited.

"It *is* such a small piece of land," she finally said. "Maybe it's not worth developing."

"There would be a nice plaque on the gate." I made up strategy as I talked. "Your name would be listed."

Amelia Drane gazed across her blue carpet, as if seeing a vision. "For years this company has been linked with progress. Now we can be champions of the past."

The woman sounded like a commercial.

"Does this mean you'll fill out the forms?"

Amelia Drane swept a rain cape over her shoulders. "Oh, yes."

"And you'll send me copies?"

She looked amused. "I promise," she said. "Don't worry, Mr. Jones, your garden is safe.

This is *excellent* publicity. We go from big, bad developers to preservers of history and nature."

Amelia Drane tucked her poofy hair into a plastic bonnet. "A time like this calls for celebration. Mr. Jones, may I take you to lunch?"

All this Mr. Jones-ing. Like I was a bigshot businessman.

"What about your appointment at eleven?" I asked.

"Oh, *that*," she replied, waving her hand.

Huh, I bet Amelia Drane had made up that appointment just to get rid of me and my briefcase.

The woman had more strategy than a bad guy in a Nemo strip. But I had faked her out.

"Lunch?" I grinned. "I know a place that has great chocolate pudding."

CHAPTER FOURTEEN

• •

Two chocolate puddings later, I caught the bus back home. The rain had stopped. The sky was as blue as Drane and Company's carpet.

Wait till I told Reuben and Juana. I could picture it now: high fives all around. Nathan Aramack would get a good news story. Mr. K. could return his gallons of dirt. Huh, I'd even help. I bet Mailbags would, too.

Maybe Mama wouldn't be too mad about me skipping school. I decided to smooth on some strategy. I would plant myself by our phone, tuck my arm round her tree. "Mama," I'd say, "you rescued a ficus. Me, I saved a whole garden."

I would probably be grounded. Mama worried when I broke the rules. But she might smile a little at my success.

High fives, dirt-toting, Mama-chatting—all that could come later. Right now I just wanted to mosey down Evert Street. Pass the blacktop. Lean on Rooter's gate.

Yeah.

V for victory.

Mission Greentop: accomplished.

I headed for my soggy plot. *Squish-squish-squish.* Mr. K.'s holes were full of muddy water.

And my bush—a puddle of thorns.

The roses, though, were still hanging on. Rain had pounded them for three whole days—but they had survived. One of those garden surprises.

Then I got another surprise.

Rolling down Evert. Built like a tank.

Blood Green.

He was forever skipping school. But why'd he have to miss the same day as me?

"Jones." Blood's mouth screwed into a smile. His arms bulged in his T-shirt.

Blood unlatched the gate and entered.

I was trapped. Surrounded by fence too high to leap.

Blood rammed through gardens.

Plowed straight toward me.

His mission: to destroy.

I held my ground, brain whirling. Maybe I could make a break for the gate. Zigzag through the garden.

No one would hear me holler for help. Kids were still in school, the blacktop empty.

Squosh. Squosh. Squosh. Blood's big shoes.

Squosh. Squosh. Through Mailbags's garden.

Blood stopped in Mr. K.'s plot.

"Jones," he said. And he lunged.

Things happened fast then. Blood stepped into a hole. Teetered.

Splot.

Face first in the mud.

He lurched to his feet like some Nemo monster.

Leaped at me again.

Slid. Right into the rosebush.

"Yow!"

Blood had jumped my fierce pile of sticks.

"Yow!" He flailed wildly. Arms, legs, stems—everything churned in the mud. Rose petals flew through the air.

Finally Blood lay still. Gripped by thorns, a mud-covered Shamu. Petals floated around him.

"Jones," he whimpered.

Talk about garden surprises.

I gazed down. What should I do?

I could leave Blood there. School would be out soon. The sidewalks would fill with kids heading home. Kids that Blood had bullied. Wouldn't they *love* to catch him like this?

I could mess with Blood the way he messed with Reuben and me.

I could haul off and hit him. He'd get a taste of what he dished out.

No, I wanted to do something that would last a loonng time.

At my feet, two eyes narrowed. "Jones," Blood spat, "you better help."

"On one condition," I said.

CHAPTER FIFTEEN

● ●

Slowly, slowly I worked the thorn from Blood's shirt.

"Hurry, man."

"Hold still," I commanded. "When you thrash around, the thorns twist tighter. And the mud slimes everything."

"I should sue," Blood grumbled.

Listen to the boy. All that big talk? Nothing but air.

"One down," I said, moving to the next thorn. "About twenty to go."

"Faster," Blood demanded.

I had to smile. What strategy! If Reuben was here, we'd be slapping some skin.

See, before I agreed to help, before I started on the first thorn, I had laid out the options for the big lump of mud.

1. Blood could stay trapped. Maybe kids passing by would help. Maybe not.

OR

2. He could promise to lay off Reuben and me. No punching or pushing. No "Rose Jones" or "Art Fart." No picking on Juana, Gaby, and Ro.

"If the punching starts again," I had continued, "the whole school might be *very* interested in how you lost a fight—to a rosebush."

The Blood-lump had growled.

"Reuben will draw a picture." I tapped my chin, thinking it through. "We'll pass out copies. Two or three hundred. The school newspaper would get all the details."

What could Blood do but promise?

And when I had worked my way down to the last six thorns, I knew he would keep that promise.

See, Blood liked to wear big jeans. The kind that barely hold to the hips. In the tussle, his jeans had ridden low . . . low . . . down to his knees.

The last six thorns—well, each had grabbed a chunk of Blood's underwear. They had poked and ripped and slashed.

Those thorns had whipped Blood's sorry butt.

"Huh," I said, peeling back muddy cloth. "This how you got your name?"

"Jones." Blood glared.

"*Mr.* Jones," I corrected.

• • •

It's been one month since Blood tackled my rosebush. Sometimes he still lets fly with "Bouquet Jones." I figure that boy is stuck in his pea-brain ways. It's hard for him to change.

So I just draw out the word rose to remind him. *Roosse.*

Blood shuts right up. He knows I keep my silence as long as he keeps his promise.

Mr. K. had once told me that a fall rose was special. Little did he know.

On account of Blood's whomping, Mama never did see my flowers. But I managed to save a few petals.

She mixed them into something called potpourri—shriveled plant parts stuck in a bowl.

Potpourri. Another villain for Captain Nemo.

Villains, huh. These days Blood is not the only bad guy keeping a promise. Last week Mailbags delivered a thick brown envelope. It was addressed to Mr. Jones.

Inside were copies of reports and completed forms.

There was a scrawled message on Drane and Company paper.

> *Mr. Jones,*
> *Plans moving nicely. Looking forward*
> *to dedication ceremony in the spring.*
> *A. Drane*

Dedication ceremony: a fancy name for a party.

There would be speeches and photos, maybe

cookies for all. A plaque for Drane and Company. Nathan Aramack might come with a big TV camera.

Rooter's would be safe. A teeny national park that no one could bulldoze or build on. The mishmash of plots would continue.

Including Plot 5-1, which grows the best weeds in the city. I forked my fingers: *V* for victory.

Yeah, a lot had happened in the past month.

In fact, I had just finished being grounded. No after-school b-ball, no hanging out with Reuben. My mama had grounded me so long I felt stuck as a seed in the dirt.

"You skipped school," she told me a month ago. "You went downtown by yourself."

"But, Mama!" I had tried smoothing on strategy.

"Don't even *try* your fast talk with me." Mama's worry frown had been deep. "Just because things turned out okay doesn't make this behavior right. Understand?"

Yeah, I guessed I understood. Mama didn't want me getting hurt or lost. She didn't want me growing super-sneaky, like Amelia Drane.

At first, Reuben and Juana had been mad at me for tackling Drane and Company without them. But when they saw my stuck-seed, bored state, they got over it. At school, Reuben told me he was working on Nemo's weirdest villian yet.

"Draneco has a bubble head and a shiny cape." He smiled. "She's scarier than the Unspeakable Z."

Uh-oh, the Unspeakable Z. Zucchini. Maybe Mailbags and Mr. K. could plant less the next spring. Then there'd be no extra to pass on to Mama. No zucchini baked, boiled, breaded, or fried.

I had till April to figure a strategy.

But the Unspeakable Z was to return sooner. Much sooner.

• • •

On my first Friday freed from grounding, Reuben and I moseyed home from school. I didn't even mind moving poke-turtle slow, like Reuben. My man and I needed time to plan the perfect Saturday.

Tomorrow we'd play a little one-on-one at

the blacktop. Work on our latest Nemo strip. Even help Mr. K. fill in his holes. I'd already given my five cups of rich dirt to the ficus, I told Reuben. Gift from the garden.

"Jackson grows roses. Jackson grows roses. Big, red, smelly-good ROOSSES."

I whipped around.

"What?" asked Gaby, all innocent. "I can sing. It's a free country."

"How about 'Twinkle, Twinkle'?" Juana suggested.

"Boring," said Gaby.

"Baby song," sniffed Ro.

Why did I make Blood promise not to deck those two? I thought, rounding the corner.

That's when I saw it.

Huge, hulking, green.

I blinked. Zucchini on wheels.

Mama patted it proudly.

Juana giggled. Gaby and Ro made straight for the parked monster.

"Sure is bright" was all Reuben said.

My plant doctor mama had done it. She'd gotten a green ambulance.

One of her teachers had recommended her

for a job, Mama told us. Two offices needed regular plant care.

"This new work is part-time." Mama's eyes were all shiny-happy. "I can do it before my regular job. Think, Jackson, a little extra money. And the start of my own business."

Mama had traded our car for a van. She had needed more space to carry her tools.

Mailbags pulled up behind Mama's van. His mail truck hunkered small as a peanut beside a green zuke.

"Nice rig." He smiled.

Mama smiled back, flourishing open a door. "Who wants a ride?"

Gaby and Ro scrambled in.

"Jackson," they yelled, "now we can go EVERYWHERE with you."

Juana hopped inside, followed by Reuben. Even Mailbags took a seat. Their heads bobbed together like a bunch of wildflowers. *Wild* flowers, to be exact.

Mama touched my arm. "What do you think?"

I eyeballed the van. I lived in a jungle,

talked to a tree. Now I had to ride in a vegetable.

"Mama," I said, "my life is getting too
green."

Mama nodded seriously. "I've thought hard
about all your help, Jackson. And how my
studies have taken over."

Where was *this* headed?

"I plan to take just one class from now
on till I finish," Mama went on. "Free up
some time. Can't have you being a guy
Cinderella."

My feelings exactly.

Mama and I slapped skin. She didn't do it
right. But she tried.

"When I cook, you can clean," I suggested.

"Starting tonight." Mama smiled.

I climbed into the van, very cool. "I know
the *perfect* first job for your van."

"That so?" Mama started the engine.

I nodded. "Let me show you the way."

Down the street were *gallons* of dirt.
Reuben and I had planned to tote them tomorrow. But with a van and all these helping
hands—why not do it today?

Gaby started in on her Jackson-grows-red-roses song.

I grinned. Wait till Mr. K. saw us. Arriving in Mama's zucchini-mobile.

A garden surprise, for sure.

AUTHOR'S NOTE

During World War II, nearly 20 million Americans planted vegetable gardens to help provide adequate food for those at home and U.S. soldiers overseas. These victory gardens came in all shapes and sizes. They were planted in window boxes, vacant city lots, backyards, and schoolyards. With so many fathers, uncles, and older brothers away at war, the children in many households helped sow seeds, tend plants, and harvest and preserve produce. They grew carrots, turnips, spinach, tomatoes, and many other vegetables and fruits.

Most of these gardens disappeared after the war—but a few continue to flourish. They might be considered living history, a testimony to the idea that history is made not just by presidents and generals but also by ordinary children, women, and men. For years, my husband and I tended a plot in our city community garden (the Melvin Hazen Community Garden in northwest Washington, D.C.). This garden began as a victory garden and is now part of Rock Creek Park, one of the largest urban national parks in the United States. Whenever I planted, weeded, and munched home-grown lettuce and radishes there, I thought about the numerous others who had worked this same small plot of land.

ACKNOWLEDGMENTS

With much gratitude to the DC Commission on the Arts and Humanities under the National Endowment for the Arts, for a creative writing grant during the time this book was written. Thank you to Elizabeth Judd and Annie Thacher for sharing gardening thoughts, and to the Melvin Hazen Community Garden in Washington, D.C., for many good gardening years. Thank you to Kevin Mohs for kindly answering questions related to an earlier draft. Many, many thanks to Leslie Buhler, executive director, and Jill Sanderson, education director, for information on Tudor Place, a historic house and garden in Washington, D.C. I am also deeply grateful to Nancy McCoy, education director of the National Museum of American History, for insights on victory gardens and the National Park Service, and to Perry Wheelock, Rock Creek Park's cultural historian, for information on the community gardens in this national park. Big thank-you bouquets go to Jen Carlson, Jennifer Wingertzahn, and Françoise Bui for seeing the manuscript through, and to Christopher and Christy David for their continued support and good cheer.

ABOUT THE AUTHOR

Mary Quattlebaum is an award-winning author of picture books, poetry, and novels for children, including *Underground Train, Grover G. Graham and Me,* and *Jackson Jones and the Puddle of Thorns,* winner of the first Marguerite de Angeli Prize, the *Parenting* Reading Magic Award, and other accolades. She writes frequently for the *Washington Post* and teaches creative writing in Washington, D.C., where she lives with her husband and daughter. For years Mary Quattlebaum tended a plot in a city community garden, where, like Jackson Jones, she found both weeds and good fellowship.

You can read more about the author at her Web site, www.maryquattlebaum.com.